NURSERY RHYME
RAINBOW

Alison Jay

templar publishing

Painting on a rainy day,
everything looks dull and **grey**…

and something that's not very nice,
is happening to the Three Blind Mice.

Little Boy **Blue**'s asleep in the hay,
so his sheep and his cow
have both run away.

She may be short and she may be stout,
but this **yellow** teapot's the best at pouring out.

Miss Muffet's
scared of the big
black spider,
but he only wanted
to sit beside her.

Ladybird's house is fiery **red**…

but luckily all of her children have fled.

Little Bo Peep left her
white sheep alone,
but she's over
the moon that
they're finally home.

The Owl and the Pussycat set to sea...

in a beautiful boat as **green** as a pea.

It's not a good time for the Hickory Clock...

the little **brown** mouse gave him rather a shock!

Old Mother Hubbard loves to share...

but her bright **orange** cupboard is totally bare.

Jill went to
fetch water from
Turquoise Well…

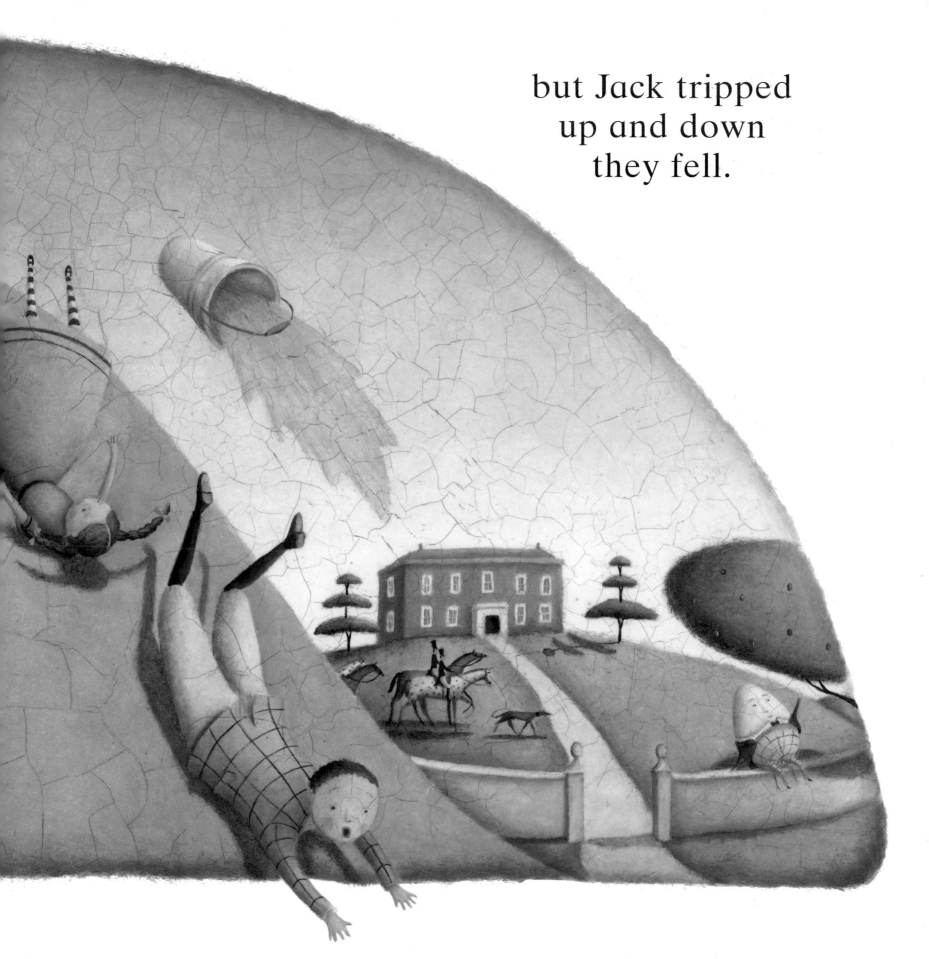

but Jack tripped
up and down
they fell.

Poor Humpty's **purple** from his fall –

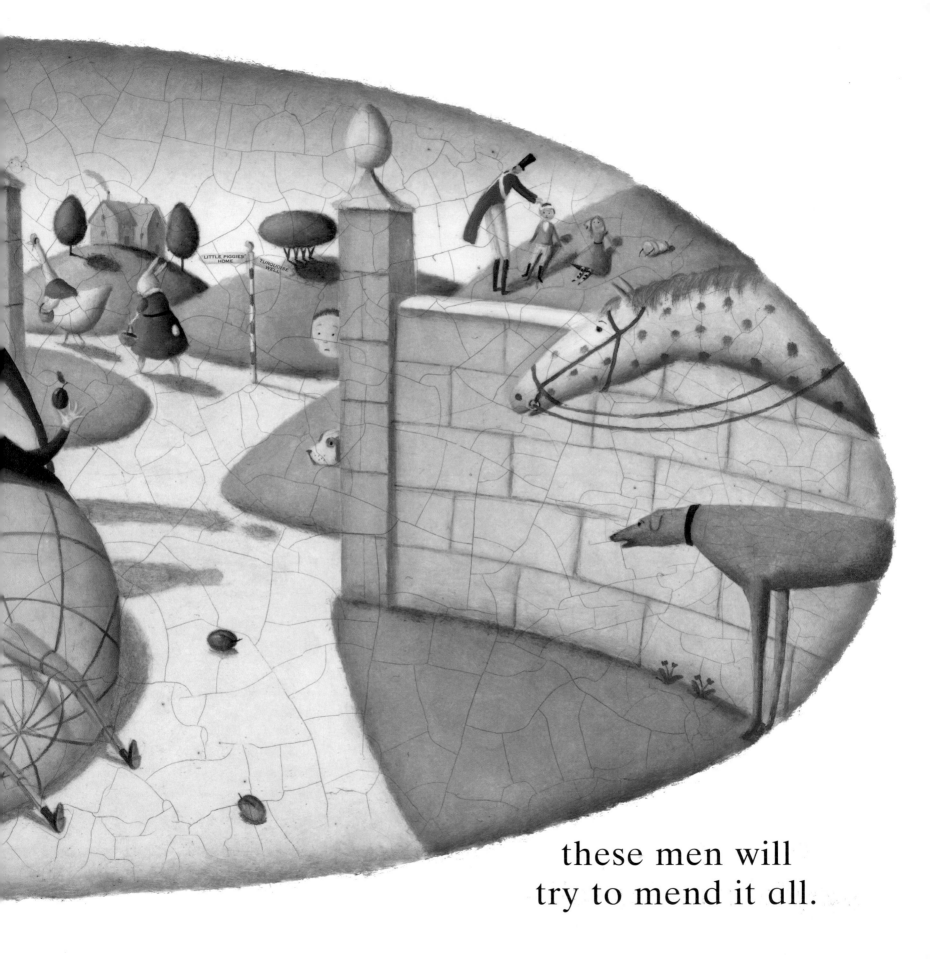

these men will
try to mend it all.

Though five **pink** piggies all love to eat,
who's not getting a roast beef treat?

In the magical light of a **silver** moon,
watch swift little Dish run away
with her Spoon.

In the **golden** palace of Old King Cole,
everybody is a merry old soul!

The Nursery Rhyme
Rainbow has come
to play...

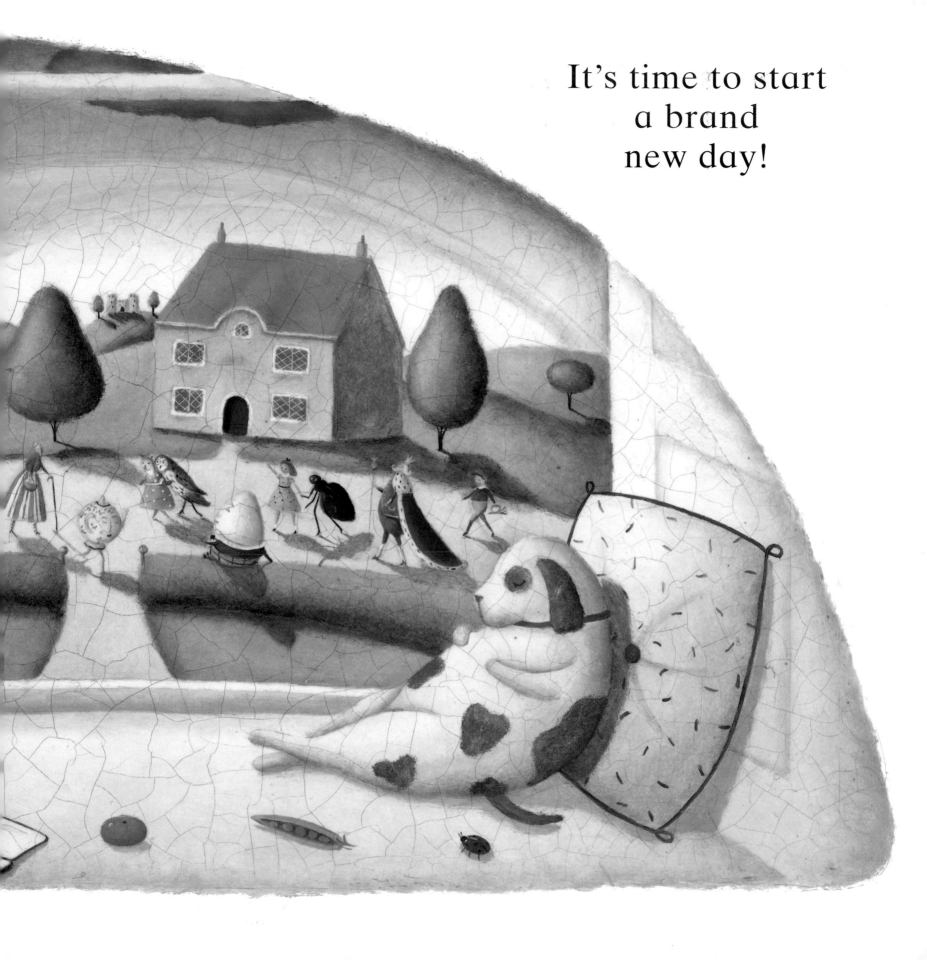

It's time to start
a brand
new day!

HOW MANY NURSERY RHYMES DID YOU SPOT?

THREE BLIND MICE

LITTLE BOY BLUE

I'M A LITTLE TEAPOT

LITTLE MISS MUFFET

LADYBIRD, LADYBIRD

LITTLE BO PEEP

THE OWL AND THE PUSSYCAT

HICKORY, DICKORY, DOCK

OLD MOTHER HUBBARD

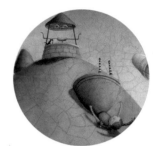

JACK AND JILL

HUMPTY DUMPTY

THIS LITTLE PIGGY

HEY DIDDLE, DIDDLE

OLD KING COLE

SING A SONG OF SIXPENCE

POLLY PUT THE KETTLE ON

BAA, BAA, BLACK SHEEP

OLD MOTHER GOOSE

RUB-A-DUB-DUB

THERE WAS AN OLD WOMAN WHO LIVED IN A SHOE

FOR MARGARET
AND JOHN HINKS,
THANK YOU FOR ALL
YOUR ENTHUSIASM,
LOVE ALISON J.

A TEMPLAR BOOK
First published in the UK in 2009 by Templar Publishing
This softback edition published in 2010 by Templar Publishing,
an imprint of The Templar Company Limited,
The Granary, North Street, Dorking, Surrey, RH4 1DN, UK
www.templarco.co.uk

Illustration copyright © 2009 by Alison Jay
Text and design copyright © 2009 by The Templar Company Limited

ISBN: 978-1-84877-309-7

Designed by Lise Tratt • Concept and words by Libby Hamilton

Printed in China